BURIED IN THE BACKYARD

by Gail Herman
illustrated by Jerry Smath

The Kane Press
New York

Acknowledgements: Our thanks to Larry D. Agenbroad, Professor of Geology, Northern Arizona University; and Kathy Anderson, Exhibit Coordinator and Webmaster, The Mammoth Site, Hot Springs, SD for helping us make this book as accurate as possible.

Book Design/Art Direction: Edward Miller

Library of Congress Cataloging-in-Publication Data

Herman, Gail, 1959-
  Buried in the backyard / by Gail Herman ; illustrated by Jerry Smath.
    p. cm. — (Science solves it!)
Summary: While trying to dig a swimming pool in their backyard, Ryan and Katie discover what they think is a dinosaur bone.
  ISBN 1-57565-126-2 (alk. paper)
  [1. Woolly mammoth—Fiction. 2. Brothers and sisters—Fiction.] I.
Smath, Jerry, ill. II. Title. III. Series.
  PZ7.H4315 Bu 2003
  [E]—dc21
                                                                    2002010660

10 9 8 7 6 5 4 3 2 1

First published in the United States of America in 2003 by The Kane Press.
Printed in Hong Kong.

Science Solves It! is a trademark of The Kane Press.

"All you want to do is read about dinosaurs!" Katie said.

Ryan smiled. "Dinosaurs are amazing!"

"But it's summer," Katie told him. "We should be outside doing something fun!"

3

"I'd only go outside if we could swim," Ryan said. "And the town pool is closed."

"Hmmm," Katie said. "What a great idea!"

"What idea?" Ryan asked her.

Katie grinned. "We need a pool!"

Ryan put down his book.

"Mom! Dad!" Katie and Ryan raced into the kitchen. "Can we have a pool in our backyard?"

"A swimming pool?" their mother asked. "That costs too much money."

Their dad laughed. "Way too much. The only way we'd get a pool is if we dug it ourselves." He laughed harder.

Katie pulled Ryan out of the room. "That's it," she whispered. "We'll dig our own pool."

Ryan looked at her like she was crazy. "You know Dad was kidding. Don't you?"

"Sure," Katie said. "But that doesn't mean we can't do it!"

"Where are the shovels?" Ryan asked.

Katie and Ryan went right to work. They dug near the blueberry bushes. Deeper and deeper. It was hard work. But the hole got bigger and bigger.

Thunk! All at once, Katie's shovel struck something hard. "It must be a rock," Ryan said.

Katie dug some more. She peered down the hole. "It's not a rock."

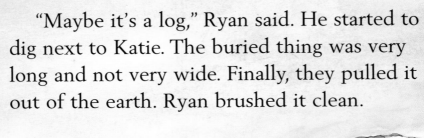

"Maybe it's a log," Ryan said. He started to dig next to Katie. The buried thing was very long and not very wide. Finally, they pulled it out of the earth. Ryan brushed it clean.

"It's a bone!" said Katie.

"Wow!" Ryan said. "It's almost as tall as I am. It must belong to a big animal."

"Like a horse," Katie agreed.

"Or maybe . . ." Ryan caught his breath. "A dinosaur!"

Katie laughed. "A dinosaur bone? In our backyard? You're dreaming."

"Oh, yeah?" Ryan said. He was already heading for the house. "I'm getting a tape measure!" he yelled.

"Four feet! See?" said Ryan. "It could be a dinosaur bone. Let's take it to the museum and look at the dinosaur skeletons!"

"They won't let us in there with a huge bone," Katie said.

"Sure they will," Ryan told her. "Kids bring lots of stuff there. Besides, the lady at the entrance knows me."

"I'll bet she does," said Katie.

Ryan was right. They walked
into the museum with no trouble at all.

"I know where the dinosaurs are," Ryan said.

"Big surprise," Katie muttered.

They passed exhibit after exhibit. Ryan was
so excited, he didn't look at a thing. He didn't
even stop to tie a loose shoelace.

"Oops!" Ryan tripped.
The bone nearly fell.
"Great save," Katie said.
Ryan straightened up. He was eye to
eye with more bones. He gasped. "Katie!
This is what we've got!"

The **Woolly Mammoth** was a long-ago relative of the elephant.

Spine

Skul

Ribs

Foot

Thigh bone

Katie read the sign. "Woolly mammoth." She nudged Ryan. "See? I told you it wasn't a dinosaur!"

"So what!" Ryan said. "This is a prehistoric animal, too! It lived way after the dinosaurs but still, thousands and thousands of years ago."

"Really?" Katie said. "In our backyard!"

65 Million Years Ago Dinosaurs Became Extinct

About **5** to **2** Million Years

First Humans

There were different kinds of mammoths, but the best known is the **Woolly Mammoth**. An adult weighed between **12,000** and **16,000** pounds, about the same as a school bus.

"Yep," Ryan said. "Woolly mammoths lived around the same time as the first humans—during the Ice Age."

"The what?" Katie asked.

Ryan waved toward a door. "Follow me."

3½ Million to 10,000 Years Ago | 10,000 Years —— to — Today

First Mammoths

Woolly Mammoths

Pyramids of Egypt

Last Woolly Mammoths Die Out

ice age

About two million years ago, thick sheets of ice called glaciers moved across the land. It was freezing cold. In some places, snow stayed on the ground all year long.

"The Ice Age was cool," Ryan said.
"You mean COLD," Katie told him.
Ryan grinned. "That, too."
"What if we'd been alive back then?"
Katie asked.

Mammoth Bone Hut

What can you do with a mammoth bone?
Early humans built homes with them—mostly
in parts of Russia where few trees grew. But
that's not all. They made bones into furniture,
tools like shovels and fishhooks, weapons,
and even jewelry. Plus, they ate mammoth
meat and warmed up with mammoth fur!

"Maybe we would have been mammoth hunters," Ryan said. "And we'd have cooked mammoth meat for dinner."

"Or," said Katie, "maybe we would have had a pet mammoth—or even two!"

"I don't think so," said Ryan.

"Excuse me." A guard stood over Ryan and Katie. "Where did you get that bone?"

"We brought it with us!" Katie said quickly. "We found it in our backyard."

"Well!" The guard grinned. "I think you should meet our scientists!"

That same day Dr. Hook came to Ryan and Katie's house. She talked to their parents about mammoths and the Ice Age and how much she wanted to dig for more bones in their backyard.

Lots of scientists came back a few days
later. Shovels flew. Machines dug.

One scientist yelled, "Look at this!" He
had found a mammoth tusk. It was very
long. Katie and Ryan helped measure it.

"Ten feet! Wow!" Ryan said.

"What did they use their tusks for?" Katie asked.

"To fight with," the scientist said, "and to poke through snow and ice to find grass. Mammoths ate 400 pounds of plants every day!"

"That's a lot of salad!" Ryan said.

How Do You Dig Up Fossils? Big machines and tools are used first. As soon as scientists see fossils in the dirt, they switch to smaller tools. Wood frames and markers help keep track of where each fossil is found.

Another scientist found a tooth. It was as big as a shoebox!

"Adult mammoths had four teeth at a time," he told the kids. "When a tooth wore out, a new one grew in its place."

A mammoth grew six sets of teeth during its life. When the last set wore out, the mammoth could no longer chew. So it died.

Ryan and Katie spent hours and hours at the dig. One day Dr. Hook hurried over to them.

"I have exciting news," she said. "It looks as if there's a whole mammoth skeleton right here in your backyard!"

25

The next day *everybody* learned about the discovery. Katie and Ryan were on TV! So were their mom and dad.

CHILDREN FIND MAMMOTH SKELETON

When the cameras stopped rolling, Mom looked at the kids. "After this, we're going to have a giant hole in the ground," she said. "What do you think we should do with it?"

It wasn't long before Katie was splashing in their brand-new pool.

"Come on in," she called to Ryan.

Ryan peered over his book. He gazed at the pool. It was like a giant watering hole. A place where woolly mammoths would have come long, long ago. He could almost see them.

What killed the mammoths? More changes in the weather? Grassy plains turning into forests, so the mammoths could not feed? Human hunters? Sickness? Nobody knows for sure.

REST IN PEACE

"Ryan!" Katie called. "All you want to do is read about woolly mammoths! Come on in."

Ryan smiled. It *was* kind of hot. So he jumped in, too.

THINK LIKE A SCIENTIST

Ryan thinks like a scientist—and so can you!
Scientists measure. For instance, they try to find out
how long or short, heavy or light, hot or cold things are.
They use measuring tools, like scales and thermometers.

Look Back

On page 9, how does Ryan estimate the length of the
bone? On page 11, what tool does Ryan use to measure
the bone? What does his answer say about how tall
Ryan is?

Try This!

How long are the bones in your legs?
Work with a friend.
(Remember to record the measurements.)
Hold a tape measure on the outside of your friend's leg.
Measure from the top of the leg to the spot where the
knee begins. How long is your friend's upper leg bone?
Next, measure the lower leg bone from the knee to the
ankle. How long is that bone?

Now it's your friend's turn
to measure *your* leg bones.
Compare measurements.
What did you find out?

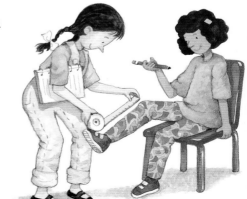